The Vampire's Coffin

I carefully placed my fingers under the lid of the coffin and began to lift. I prayed it wouldn't squeak. Suddenly the lid jumped up all by itself! A hand shot out and closed over mine! I shrieked and tried to jump back, but the powerful grip tightened and pulled me closer.

"Help! Help!" I screamed, as I realized with horror that I was going to be pulled into the coffin with the vampire.

Books by Drew Stevenson

The Case of the Horrible Swamp Monster
The Case of the Visiting Vampire

Available from MINSTREL Books

The Case of the Visiting VAMPIRE

DREW STEVENSON

illustrated by
SUSAN SWAN

PUBLISHED BY POCKET BOOKS

New York London Toronto Sydney Tokyo

This novel is a work of fiction. Names, characters, places and incidents are either the product of the author's imagination or are used fictitiously. Any resemblance to actual events or locales or persons, living or dead, is entirely coincidental.

A Minstrel Book published by
POCKET BOOKS, a division of Simon & Schuster Inc.
1230 Avenue of the Americas, New York, NY 10020

Published by arrangement with Dodd, Mead & Company
Library of Congress Catalog Card Number: 86-16583

ISBN: 0-671-65732-1

First Minstrel Books printing October 1988

10 9 8 7 6 5 4 3 2 1

Printed in the U.S.A.

THIS BOOK IS DEDICATED TO

THE PRICES, WHO MADE ME THEIR THIRD SON,

AND

THE HUGHEYS, WHO MADE ME THEIR SECOND.

"There are monsters,
and we'll catch one yet."
—J. Huntley English, M.H.

1

It was dark. The horrible vampire was walking slowly toward me. As he got closer, I could see the deadly fangs in his red mouth.

I wanted to run, but I couldn't. I wanted to scream, but I couldn't. I was so scared I couldn't do anything but watch his hands reaching for my neck.

With his cold fingers touching my skin, I finally did scream. I screamed and screamed and screamed.

And then the lights went on.

"Enough already!" Verna Wilkes cried from the front row, where she was holding her hands over her ears.

The vampire let go of my throat. I blinked and looked around. I'd been so caught up in the part I was playing I had forgotten I wasn't really a prisoner in Castle Dracula. I was Raymond Almond, and I was standing on the stage of the Big Lake Theater in Barkley, Pennsylvania, auditioning for a part in a play.

Next to me, Bill Chambers took off the vampire mask and the big gloves he'd been wearing. "Sure is hot under that thing," he complained.

Verna, meanwhile, was sitting there looking at me as if she had ordered a cheeseburger and gotten a bowl of mashed carrots instead.

"You sounded like a cat fight," she sneered.

"Oh, yeah?" I responded. "I'll have you know I've been screaming for weeks. I got so good at it that Dad made me do my practicing in the woods."

"And that's just where an actor of your talent belongs," Verna said with a snicker. "In the woods."

All the kids who were sitting in the audience waiting to audition laughed. I gave Verna a look that would have made Dracula himself proud. Verna Wilkes is the bossiest, most stuck-up kid I ever met. Wouldn't you know that, of all the kids trying out for the part, Verna was the one auditioning right after me?

I turned to Bill. "Why don't you put on your vampire mask and bite her neck?"

"I heard that, Raymond!" Verna growled, clenching her fists.

"All right, that's enough," Peggy Love said, as she joined us onstage. Peggy is on the board of directors of the Big Lake Theater and had volunteered to help us kids with our auditions.

"Fighting won't make this go any faster," she reminded us. "And, by the way, Raymond, you scream very well."

"Thank you," I beamed, jumping down off the stage.

The lights dimmed as I walked up the aisle to the exit. I would have hung around to see how good

Verna and the rest of my competition were but I had a date to meet a friend for ice cream.

Suddenly, a blood-curdling sound almost blew me out the door. My first thought was that someone had stuck a pin in an elephant. Then I realized it was Verna doing her audition onstage. I should have known that anyone with a mouth as big as Mount St. Helens could scream like a pro. I knew then and there—Verna was going to get the part!

As I walked sadly away from the theater, that crisp fall evening, I had no way of knowing that soon I would be up to my skinny neck in something that would have me screaming for real.

2

I thought about the play as I walked along the road leading back to the center of town. The Big Lake Theater's newest offering was *The Count of Castle Dracula.* Whenever the BLT puts on a production, actors from all over the Pittsburgh area audition for parts. Dr. Mark Stevens, a drama professor at Chatham College in Pittsburgh, had been asked to direct this play. But the news that had everyone really excited was that a real professional actor from Europe was going to have the lead role of Count Dracula. Even more exciting—there was a part in the play for a kid my age! Whichever kid was chosen would not only get to be in the play but would get paid for it as well.

When I was in second grade I'd played Terrible Tooth Decay in a class skit on how to brush your teeth. Verna had played the part of Squeaky Clean Gums. She had swept me off the stage with a giant toothbrush. Acting has been in my blood ever since. I had never been in a real play before, and I'd had my heart set on being in this one.

The Big Lake Theater sits beside a not-so-big lake on the edge of the not-so-big town of Barkley. It didn't take me long to walk downtown. The neon sign of Majersky's Ice Cream Parlor was lit up like a milk-shake oasis in the night. I planned to drown my disappointment in a strawberry soda with chocolate ice cream. Maybe two of them, if that's what it took.

I stepped into the friendly warmth and walked over to a kid with thick glasses who was sitting at a corner table. He was as short and chunky as I was tall and skinny.

"Hi, Hunt," I said, joining him.

"Hello, Raymond," Huntley replied. "How did your audition go?"

"Not so good," I said sadly. "Did you know that Verna Wilkes can scream louder than a herd of pigs in the Grand Canyon?"

Huntley shook his head in sympathy as a waitress took our order.

"You said on the phone you had something to show me," I reminded him.

Huntley pulled a small white card out of his pocket and handed it to me. In fancy black lettering it read:

> **J. Huntley English, M.H.**
> *Investigator of Unexplained Phenomena*
>
> *Write:* 665 Copper Kettle Rd.
> Barkley, PA 14850
>
> *Call:* 412-853-4432

"I just had these business cards printed up," he said.

I should explain here that Huntley has this thing about monsters. He's fascinated with them. He believes in them. And he's determined to have a close encounter with one. The M.H. stands for Monster Hunter. Huntley adds it to his name the way doctors add M.D. to theirs. Huntley is very proud of being an M.H. He says there are very few monster hunters in the world. He's certainly the only one in Barkley.

I give Huntley a lot of credit. Being a monster hunter isn't easy when you live in Pennsylvania. Scotland has the Loch Ness Monster. The Pacific Northwest has Bigfoot. Tibet has the Abominable Snowman. New York has Champ. All we have in Barkley is Verna Wilkes. But if there *is* a stray monster lurking around here somewhere, Huntley will be the one to find it.

"Very impressive, Hunt," I said.

"Thank you, Raymond." He beamed at me. "I wanted you to be the first to have one."

The waitress brought our treats and, between draws on our straws, Huntley filled me in on the latest monster news. He told me about a recent UFO sighting near Winchester, Virginia, and a house haunting in Lincoln, Nebraska. I knew he was disappointed nothing like that was happening here.

All too soon it was time to go home. I say that because Huntley may be one of my best friends but I don't usually get to see him all that much. If he went to the regular public school we'd be in the same seventh-grade class. But Huntley is super smart and is in a special program for gifted kids in Pittsburgh. Not many people in Barkley even know he exists. Those that do usually think he's weird. Even I have to admit he's a little strange sometimes. But that's why I like him. He's different from everyone else I know. He likes being a loner, but he also likes having me for his friend. That makes me feel good.

After we waved good-bye, I looked at his business card again. I remembered how last spring Verna and I had called him in to solve what we now call "The Case of the Horrible Swamp Monster." I figured after that I would never need the services of a monster hunter again.

As usual, I had figured wrong.

3

Several days later I got a call from Peggy Love. She was phoning all the kids who'd auditioned to thank them for trying out and to tell them she had chosen Verna for the part.

"Don't be upset, Raymond," Peggy tried to console me. "There will be other plays and other auditions."

"I know," I said, "but I really wanted to be in *this* play. With a real actor from Europe going to be in it and everything."

"It is exciting," Peggy admitted. "Especially when

you consider he's from Romania. That's behind the Iron Curtain, you know."

"Is he coming all the way here just to be in the play?" I wondered.

Peggy laughed. "Goodness, no. His name is Bela Mezgar and he's in Pittsburgh as the artist in residence of Chatham College. He'll be on campus all semester, lecturing on theater and performing. It was great of him to take time out from his busy schedule to be in our play. He's perfect for the part. We're delighted the way everything turned out."

"Looks like everyone's delighted but me," I muttered after I hung up.

The first rehearsal of *The Count of Castle Dracula* was held the second Monday in October at the Big

Lake Theater. I was surprised when Verna came up to me the next day at school. She usually makes a point of ignoring me.

"Listen closely, Raymond," she whispered in my ear. "I want you to meet me at the BLT tonight after rehearsal."

"Why?" I said, sounding as cool as I could. "You got the part."

"Forget the part," she hissed. "I want you there. Something strange is going on."

"My parents won't let me out late on a school night," I said grumpily.

"You won't be out late," Verna promised. "My Mom is picking me up afterward. She'll give you a ride home."

"Why do you always want me around when something strange is going on?" I complained. "And don't say it's because *I'm* strange. What is going on, anyway?"

"Just meet me there tomorrow night after rehearsal," she said as she walked away. "You'll see for yourself."

It sounded like a threat. Which is why I considered not going. But I knew I would. I was dying to know what she was talking about. Verna's the kind of person who will walk through a cemetery alone after dark if it will get her home quicker. She doesn't scare easily.

And if Verna Wilkes says something strange is going on, then you'd better believe it's something *really* strange.

4

Verna and I go back a long way. I first met her in kindergarten. I had just finished building a tower out of blocks when she came along and knocked it down with a toy dump truck. If Verna were a spider, I'd be a fly. And yet there I was, walking out to the Big Lake Theater that night just like she wanted.

When I got to the BLT, there were still a lot of cars in the parking lot, so I knew rehearsal wasn't over yet. To kill time, I walked down the lawn to the lake. There was a beautiful moon out. I sat on one of the benches for awhile and watched it twinkle on the rippling waters. Then I stood up, stretched, and headed slowly back up the hill.

The BLT looked grand in the moonlight. It's a huge brick building with stained-glass windows. It was built back in the 1950's by a wealthy banker who donated it to the community. People from all over western Pennsylvania, and even West Virginia and Ohio, have been enjoying productions there ever since.

I was halfway up the lawn when I got the feeling I wasn't alone. I looked ahead in time to see a figure duck into some shrubbery. Verna! I figured she was going to jump out at me as I walked by and scare me half to death. Verna's good at that sort of thing.

I pretended I hadn't noticed and kept walking. But as I passed the shrubs, I turned and leaped into them. I had wanted to turn the tables on Verna. As usual, I turned the tables on myself.

Verna wasn't there. A man was. He was short and stocky, but not fat. He looked hard and solid in his dark blue suit. What stuck in my mind were the glasses he was wearing. They had silver metal frames that reflected the moonlight.

The man wasn't even startled by my sudden arrival. He just stood there looking at me.

"I'm sorry. I thought you were someone else," I babbled nervously. "I think I hear my mother calling so I'd better go now."

I didn't waste any time getting out of there and up to the parking lot. Rehearsal was over and the lot was filled with people and moving cars. Before stepping in the door of the theater, I looked back down at the shrubs. No one was in sight.

Strange things were starting to happen and I hadn't even talked to Verna yet.

5

The theater was dark except for a few scattered lights. Verna was alone on the stage. I joined her and began to tell her about the man outside in the bushes.

"Never mind outside," she snapped. "There's someone I want you to see inside."

Suddenly a man appeared from the shadows. It was as if he materialized out of thin air. Even Verna jumped a little. The man seemed just as startled to find us standing there.

"Hello, Mr. Mezgar." I could tell Verna was trying to sound cheerful. "This is Raymond Almond."

Bela Mezgar was tall and thin, but he looked plenty strong. His jet-black hair was combed straight back and was the same color as his cape, which hung down almost to the floor. His complexion was so pale it made his dark eyes seem ready to pop out. I found myself staring into them as if I were hypnotized. Slowly he held out a long arm and I shook his hand. His skin was cold and clammy to the touch. I pulled my fingers away as soon as I could.

"It is a pleasure to meet you, Raymond," he said in a deep voice. Though he had a strong accent, his English was very good.

All I could do in reply was nod my head.

"I must be going," he said solemnly. "Good evening to you both."

He turned and disappeared into the darkness as suddenly as he had appeared.

"That guy gives me the creeps," I said with a shiver.

"Me, too," Verna admitted. "That's why I wanted you to see him."

That startled me almost as much as Bela Mezgar had. I always figured no one short of Jack the Ripper could give Verna Wilkes the creeps.

"So what's going on?" I asked.

Verna took a deep breath.

"Last night after rehearsal, I went out into the lobby to get a drink from the water fountain. While I was there, I heard someone drop a coin in the pay phone around the corner. Then I heard Mr. Mezgar's voice. I didn't mean to listen but . . ."

Verna fell silent.

"All right," I prodded her. "You didn't mean to listen but you did. What did you hear?"

"I didn't hear much. He spoke very softly, and most of what he said was in Romanian or something. But a couple of times he did say something in English."

Verna fell silent again. She was driving me nuts.

"So what did he say?"

"One time he asked, 'Is my coffin ready yet?' Another time he said, 'My one heart must die so the other may live.' "

"What do you think he meant?" I asked.

"You've heard of Transylvania, haven't you?"

"That's where Dracula was supposed to have come from."

"And where is Transylvania?"

I shook my head. "I don't know."

"It's in Romania, Raymond. In Romania."

At that point I think my heart stopped.

"And where is Bela Mezgar from?" Verna went on.

"Romania," I gasped. "Are you saying he's a vampire or something?"

Verna shrugged her shoulders. "I told you what he said on the phone, and you saw what he looks like."

I reached into my pocket and handed her Huntley's new business card. Verna looked at it and nodded grimly.

6

"This room is just as strange as I remember it," Verna muttered as we stepped into Huntley's office the next day after school.

Huntley lives with his parents in a three-bedroom house. Since he's an only child, he's allowed to use the extra bedroom for his office. A dinosaur mobile hangs from an overhead light in the middle of the room. There are monster-movie posters covering the walls. The bookshelves are overflowing with horror and science fiction books. A bust of Count Dracula sits on a huge desk.

When Huntley saw me enter the room, his eyes

lit up. Then he saw Verna come in behind me and he frowned. Verna had once told him that on the Verna Wilkes Weirdness Scale he rated a perfect 10.

"Please sit down." Huntley offered us the two chairs in front of his desk.

"What do you know about vampires?" Verna got right to the point.

"I've done a lot of research on the subject," Huntley answered coolly.

"Do you believe in them?"

Huntley got a dreamy look on his face. "The legend of the vampire comes to us through the mists of time."

"We're not talking about mist," Verna growled, "and we don't have much time. Do you believe in them?"

"Of course," Huntley answered.

"Good! Let's get down to business."

She then told him about Bela Mezgar and the strange phone conversation she had overheard. When she finished, Huntley leaned back in his swivel chair and stared at the ceiling. He didn't say anything for a long while. I could almost hear Verna's teeth grinding together.

"If a vampire is indeed among us," he said at last, almost to himself, "everyone is in great danger."

I glanced nervously at Dracula's head. I could have sworn it was staring at me.

"But we must look at the evidence carefully," Huntley warned us. "Raymond? Tell me your story."

I did.

"You said Bela Mezgar looked pale?" he asked me when I finished.

"He was white as a sheet."

"And his skin was cold to the touch? And you felt hypnotized when you looked into his eyes and couldn't speak?"

I nodded.

Huntley spoke in a soft, spooky voice. "Legend says that vampires can't stand daylight. That's why they only come out at night."

"That's why he looks so pale," I whispered.

"Vampires are known as the living dead," Huntley went on. "That would account for his cold skin. Legend also says vampires have the power to hypnotize people and make them dumb."

"Raymond doesn't need a vampire to make him dumb," Verna interrupted.

Huntley ignored her.

"Vampires also have the power to steal a person's strength. When you were looking into Bela Mezgar's eyes, did you feel weak, Raymond?"

"Come to think of it, I did."

"How about what I heard him say on the phone?" Verna asked.

Huntley scratched his chin thoughtfully. "Let's see. He said: 'Is my coffin ready yet?' Vampires must return to their coffins before sunrise."

"What about the rest?" I asked breathlessly.

"He said: 'My one heart must die so the other may live.' According to a vampire book I read a few months ago, people in Eastern Europe believe that a vampire really has two hearts. Because one heart never dies, the vampire remains undead forever."

"Wait a minute!" I cried out. "This is crazy! Do you know what you're saying?"

"I'm afraid I do, Raymond." Huntley gave me a cool, monster-hunter look. "I'm saying that Bela Mezgar may indeed be a vampire. We must find out for sure."

"We?" I squeaked.

"We," Huntley answered firmly.

7

“Thirty minutes to V.F.O.T.,” Huntley said, looking at his werewolf watch. Instead of a Mickey Mouse on the dial, Huntley’s watch has a picture of Wolfman.

“V.F.O.T.?”

“Vampire Face Off Time.”

I wish Huntley wouldn’t talk like that. For the past hour and a half we had been sitting in the public library doing our homework. Huntley was wearing his autumn monster-hunting outfit. With his long trench coat buckled at the waist and his wide-brimmed hat pulled low over his forehead, he looks like someone out of an old spy movie. When Huntley wears one of his special outfits, you know he's ready to get down to some serious monster hunting.

"I sure hope I don't faint or throw up or something," I fretted.

"You'll do just fine. So will Verna."

I remembered last spring when we had been trying to capture a monster in Lost Swamp. This big scary thing had been coming at me out of the darkness. Verna had actually jumped down from a tree onto its back! I knew right then she had more courage in her big toe than I had in my whole scrawny body.

"Time to go," Huntley said, standing up.

When we stepped outside, I shivered. I tried to pretend it was only the cold and made a big deal of zipping up my jacket. I didn't fool Huntley, though.

"Listen, Raymond," he said, as he put on his hat and tugged it down toward his eyes. "In a tight spot, there are two people I'd want by my side. Verna Wilkes is one."

"Who's the other?"

"You," he answered putting his hand on my shoulder.

I felt my spirits lift.

"Let's go for it, Hunt!"

We did a high five and headed out to the BLT. Rehearsal wasn't over, so we slipped into the auditorium and sat in the dark back row.

Bela Mezgar was onstage doing this scene where Count Dracula is alone in his castle talking to himself. He says how lonely it is being a vampire and having to live on human blood. The other actors were sitting on the floor watching him. Verna was next to Peggy Love.

As Bela Mezgar talked, I could almost believe that Count Dracula was standing there. It was great acting. But was it really an act? I looked around. All eyes were on him. Again I felt my own eyes riveted on his. I shook my head to break the spell. I couldn't afford to get hypnotized now.

Huntley was staring at him through a pair of little binoculars he had pulled out of his huge pocket. Just as I was beginning to think *he* was hypnotized, he put the binoculars down.

"He sure looks like a vampire," he whispered.

And then the scene was over. All the actors applauded. Bela Mezgar bowed.

"Great, Bela, great!" Dr. Stevens, the director, exclaimed. "That's it, gang. Good rehearsal. See you tomorrow night."

The actors gathered up their things and began leaving the theater. Huntley and I slid down in our seats so they wouldn't notice us as they filed out. Dr. Stevens followed them and dimmed the lights.

I peeked over the back of the seat in front of me. I hoped to see an empty stage. If Bela Mezgar had left, so could we. But there he was, pacing back and forth and looking at his watch.

"Okay, Raymond." Huntley nudged me. "It's time to start our Vampire Test."

With a deep breath, I stood up. As I slipped out of my seat, I tried to remember what Huntley had told us about vampires as we'd planned how to test Bela Mezgar. He'd said they hated garlic. And could never go out into daylight or they would die. He also said that vampires couldn't stand to be near a cross.

As I moved down the aisle, I wondered if I was walking toward a real bloodsucking vampire.

You've heard of having cold feet? Well, I had a cold body!

8

When I jumped up on the stage behind him, Bela Mezgar spun around so fast I could feel the breeze from his cape. He looked alarmed until he saw who it was.

"You startled me," he said. "I thought I was alone."

"I'm sorry, Mr. Mezgar," I said, trying to keep my voice calm. "We met yesterday."

"Yes, I remember. Raymond? Raymond Peanut?"

It scared me that he almost remembered my name. It's not the kind of thing you want a vampire to know.

"Almond," I reluctantly corrected him. "Raymond Almond. Right first name, wrong nut."

Bela Mezgar was staring at me with his bulging dark eyes. I tried keeping my own eyes on the huge Adam's apple that was bobbing up and down in his throat. His skin seemed almost to glow in the dim light. I was glad he didn't offer to shake my hand again as I stumbled bravely on.

"My Mom and Dad asked me to—er—invite you to our house for dinner some evening—before rehearsal. Mom said she'd make—um—spaghetti."

"Spaghetti?"

"Yeah. My Mom makes spaghetti with real homemade Italian spaghetti sauce. The kind with lots of *garlic.*"

I prayed he would accept. Huntley had said vampires can't stand garlic, so if Bela Mezgar agreed to come to our house for spaghetti with garlic sauce, it would prove he was no vampire.

It would also put me on the spot. I hadn't asked my parents if I could invite a guest for dinner. And Mom's spaghetti sauce comes out of a jar.

"No, thank you." He bowed nervously. "I am much too busy. My regrets to your parents."

That was Verna's cue to come walking on. Bela Mezgar now looked downright confused.

"I'm glad you're still here," Verna said to him

with an innocent smile. "I wanted to ask you if we could meet for lunch some day?"

Huntley had said vampires can't stand daylight and only come out at night. Therefore, if Mr. Mezgar agreed to have lunch with Verna, it would prove he was no vampire. But Bela Mezgar failed this part of the test, too.

"No, I am sorry," he answered stiffly. "My schedule will not permit it. Please excuse me now. I must return to Pittsburgh."

He turned and started quickly for the steps leading

from the stage. Just then Huntley jumped out at him from behind the curtain and thrust a silver cross up into his face. With a shriek, Bela Mezgar jumped back, holding his hands out as if to push the cross away.

"Who are you?" he yelled. "Why did you do that?" He then ran down the steps.

With our mouths hanging open, we watched him hurry up the aisle and out the back door.

Huntley was the first to speak.

"Looks like we have a vampire on our hands."

9

"Let's get out of here before he comes back," I suggested.

Huntley shook his head. "He won't come back tonight. Not as long as I have this cross. You saw how he reacted."

"All right," I said. "But what now? I say we go to Police Chief Murphy."

"And tell him what?" Huntley asked. "That the Big Lake Theater invited a real live vampire to star in their play about Dracula?"

"You're right," I admitted. "The chief would think we were crazy."

Huntley patted me on the back. "It's not easy being a believer, Raymond. I should know. I've been one all my life."

"If we can't tell anybody about this, then what *do* we do?" Verna asked.

"We stop him ourselves," Huntley answered.

"How?" Verna and I asked together.

"First I think we have to find out all we can about Mr. Bela Mezgar."

Verna thought for a moment.

"Monday night he stayed after rehearsal to make a mysterious phone call. I bet that was what he was going to do again tonight. Make another phone call."

I nodded. "If only we knew who it was he was calling."

As if to answer her, the phone in the lobby began ringing.

"Quick!" Huntley cried. "Let's answer it."

Huntley was in the lead as we ran down the stage steps and out into the lobby. When he stopped suddenly, Verna and I crashed into him. I looked up and saw old Mr. Quimbly, the BLT custodian, answering the phone. We watched as he talked for a few seconds before hanging up.

"Excuse me, Mr. Quimbly." Verna stepped forward. "Was that my mother? She's supposed to pick us up and she's late."

Mr. Quimbly shook his head.

"Sorry, Verna. It was some woman asking for Mr. Mezgar. I told her I thought he had left already. I'm about ready to lock up. If you kids need a ride, I'll be glad to drop you off in town."

We said no thank you to Mr. Quimbly's offer and walked out into the parking lot.

"That was quick thinking, Verna," Huntley said, as we waited for her mother to come. "Now we know our mystery person is a woman."

"And I bet she's someone right here in Barkley," Verna added. "That's why Mr. Mezgar calls her from the BLT. It's a local call. If he waited and called her after he goes back to Pittsburgh, it would be long distance."

"What does it all mean?" I asked the monster hunter.

"It means our vampire has his sights set on Barkley," Huntley said grimly.

"How do you figure that?" I asked, not sure I really wanted to hear the answer.

"Vampires have to return to their coffins before sunrise or die. That's why they don't like to stray far from them. Since Bela Mezgar is now staying in Pittsburgh, he must have a coffin there. A coffin isn't something you carry around with you. If he were going to be staying in Pittsburgh, he wouldn't need another coffin. But now we know that a mystery woman is building a coffin for him right here in Barkley. Verna heard him ask her if it was ready yet. I can only assume—"

"—that he's planning on spending more time here," I finished for him.

Just then Mrs. Wilkes pulled into the parking lot to pick us up. As we rode back into town, I thought about Huntley's theory. It was bad enough knowing a vampire was living in a city only thirty miles from your hometown. But the thought of having a vampire living *in* your hometown was even worse. I could almost see my mother sending me over to Bela Mezgar's house to borrow a cup of blood.

10

We didn't do any more monster hunting until Saturday afternoon. Our parents weren't too happy about our going out so much on school nights.

"I must be the only monster hunter in the world who has to deal with parents," Huntley complained.

He and I were on our way to the BLT. Verna had told us that Dr. Stevens would be there working with Mr. Pano, who was in charge of building the set for the play. Since Dr. Stevens was not only the play's director but also a professor at Chatham College, Huntley figured he'd be a good person to ask about Bela Mezgar. Verna had rehearsal that night, so she had decided to spend her afternoon playing football.

We walked down the aisle of the BLT toward a slender, pleasant-looking young man with glasses. He was onstage smoking a sweet-smelling pipe and glancing over some plans. Behind him, Mr. Pano and several workers were hammering up the background of the set, which looked like the walls of a castle. Mr. Pano owns Shorty's Lunch downtown. I waved at him and he waved back.

"Dr. Stevens?"

"Yes?"

"I'm J. Huntley English, M.H., and this is my friend Raymond Almond."

"Just call me Mark," Dr. Stevens said, shaking our hands. "What can I do for you?"

"I'm doing an article on Bela Mezgar for my school's newspaper," Huntley said, pulling a note pad and pencil out of his pocket. "May I ask you some questions?"

"Ask away."

"Let's see," Huntley began. "Mr. Mezgar is from Romania and he's in Pittsburgh as an artist in residence at Chatham College?"

Dr. Stevens nodded. "He'll be with us all semester, lecturing on theater and later performing in campus productions."

"Sounds as if he's very busy," Huntley went on. "The BLT was lucky he could find time to be in this play."

Dr. Stevens smiled. "I have to admit we *did* line up another actor to play the lead in case Bela declined. But actually Bela was quite flattered to be asked and eager to perform here. I was overjoyed! The play and the part are perfect for him."

"Did you pick it?" I asked.

"No, the choice was made by the Big Lake Theater Board of Directors. They knew that Bela would be in Pittsburgh so they chose *The Count of Castle Dracula* and gambled that they could persuade him to star in it. Their gamble paid off. It should be a great show!"

"What's Mr. Mezgar really like?" Huntley pressed on. "You know, the man behind the actor?"

"I can't help you much there," Dr. Stevens admitted. "Bela is a very private man. I do know he's a night owl."

"A night owl?"

"When he first arrived he told me he's at his best after dark. That's why we arranged all his lectures, rehearsals, and performances during evening hours. It's not unusual. A lot of actors are night people."

"But I bet they don't spend their days in coffins,"

I thought to myself. "Is he living on campus?" I asked out loud.

"No. We offered him lodgings but he preferred finding himself an apartment in the city. As I said, he's a very private man."

"I don't suppose you'd tell us where his apartment is?" Huntley asked hopefully.

Dr. Stevens smiled. "I'm afraid not, but, if you like, I'll ask him if he'll give you an interview."

We quickly declined Dr. Stevens' offer, thanked him for talking with us, and walked away up the aisle.

"Wait a minute," the director called out. "Let me ask *you* a question. You said your name is J. Huntley English, M.H. What does the M.H. stand for?"

Huntley thought for a moment. I could see he didn't want to give himself away.

"Moose Helper," Huntley called back.

We left Dr. Stevens with his mouth hanging open.

11

Huntley was unusually quiet as we walked through town. I didn't like to bother the mighty hunter while he was into some heavy thinking but . . .

"All right, what's going on in that monster brain of yours?"

Huntley looked up as if he had forgotten I was there.

"I was just thinking. Anyone who knows anything about vampireology knows that vampires need human beings to help them. Human beings who can move around during the day and do things for them. Like making sure there's always a coffin nearby."

"Why would anyone want to help a vampire?" I wondered.

"They can't help it. They're under the vampire's evil spell."

I snapped my fingers. "The mystery woman on the phone! *She* must be under Bela Mezgar's spell."

Huntley nodded. "And she's helping our vampire carry out his sinister plot."

"Plot?"

"I think Bela Mezgar arranged to get himself invited to Chatham College. And then he arranged to get himself invited to star in the BLT's autumn play. I'm betting he used the mystery woman to set everything up for him. Barkley's been his target all along. He wanted to come here without raising suspicions."

"Sounds like a lot of trouble to me," I said. "Why didn't he just come here disguised as a tourist from Romania?"

"Don't forget, Raymond, Romania is a communist country. It's behind the Iron Curtain. The citizens can't come and go as they please, the way we do. Bela Mezgar would have to have a good reason for wanting to come here or the Romanian government might not let him."

"But why does he want to come to little old Barkley, Pennsylvania, of all places?"

Huntley shook his head. "I don't know yet. Maybe we can ask our mystery woman."

"But we don't know who she is!"

"No, but I think we will soon," Huntley said, picking up the pace.

Peggy Love owns a small art print and frame shop downtown. Huntley buys most of his monster posters from her. When we walked into the store, Peggy was up on a ladder hanging a new print.

"Glad you stopped by, Huntley," she called down. "There's a new poster I think you'll like in that bin to your left."

Huntley eagerly leafed through the bin until he found a poster for the movie *The Fungus Is Among Us.* It showed a man and woman fleeing in terror from what looked like a giant green rug.

"Good thing I got my allowance today," Huntley remarked.

Peggy came down the ladder.

"By the way," Huntley said, as he paid for the poster, "I wanted to tell you how glad I am the BLT is doing *The Count of Castle Dracula.*"

Peggy smiled. "Somehow I knew you'd be pleased."

"Did you pick it? I know you're on the BLT's Board of Directors and they decide what plays to do."

Peggy shook her head. "No, I wanted to do a musical. *The Count of Castle Dracula* was Sonya Hanson's idea. She's on the board, too, you know. She heard that Bela Mezgar was coming to Pittsburgh and suggested we do a play he could be in. We agreed and, fortunately, so did Bela."

"Does Mrs. Hanson have anything to do with Chatham College?" Huntley's eyes looked wide and innocent.

"Why, yes, she does. Sonya's on the Chatham Board of Trustees."

Huntley shot me a look as we thanked Peggy and left.

"Sonya Hanson is our mystery woman," he said, when we were outside. "She's on both the College and BLT boards. Bela Mezgar must have forced her to use her influence to get Chatham to invite him to the United States. Then he made her use her influence on the BLT board to put on a play he could star in here in Barkley."

I didn't say anything. I didn't know Mrs. Hanson very well. She hasn't lived in Barkley long. She's a middle-aged lady with short gray hair and a friendly smile. She sure didn't look like a vampire helper.

And then I remembered she had an accent just like Bela Mezgar's! And she lived alone in a big house at the edge of Lost Woods. Lost Woods is a thick, dark, spooky forest that slopes down to Lost Swamp. If ever there was a good place to hide a vampire's coffin, it was there!

12

Later that night, Huntley and I picked up a double pepperoni pie at Patsy's Pizza and took it to his house. Huntley has a TV in his office, so we settled down to watch his favorite program, Chiller Theater. Wouldn't you know, the show's host, Chilly Billy, had chosen a vampire movie?

As Huntley lifted the lid of the pizza box, I pulled a small jar out of my pocket.

"What's that?" he asked.

"Garlic powder. Since you told me vampires can't stand garlic, I've been sprinkling it on just about everything I eat. You can't be too safe."

"Good idea, Raymond."

"Yeah, but it's not easy," I pointed out as I shook powder all over the pizza. "Yesterday I had to eat a peanut-butter, jelly, and garlic sandwich."

We settled back to watch the movie. It was your typical vampire flick. At the end, the handsome hero was chasing the vampire, who turned into a bat and flew off to his castle. The hero followed him and caught him in his coffin. We watched as the hero picked up a mallet and a stake and . . .

"Huntley!" I said. "No matter how evil Bela Mezgar is, I can't drive a stake through his heart or anything like that."

"Nor can I, Raymond," Huntley said, to my great relief. "I've devoted my life to studying monsters. Not to destroying them."

"But we have to do something!" I cried. "We can't just let him go around sucking the life out of people."

"We can't and we won't. What we have to do is gather proof that he's really a vampire. Then we take that proof to Police Chief Murphy and let him take it from there."

I was still plenty scared, but Huntley's plan at least sounded better than turning Bela Mezgar into a vampire shish kabob.

Just then we heard the doorbell ring, and a moment later Verna came bursting into the office. Her face was red and she was breathing hard.

"I was hoping you'd be here," she panted. "I've got news. Big news."

"What is it?" Huntley jumped to his feet.

"The coffin! I found the coffin!"

13

"You went out to Sonya Hanson's house?" I asked in amazement.

"Mrs. Hanson?" Verna looked puzzled. "What does she have to do with this?"

"Never mind that now," Huntley interjected. "Tell us your story, Verna."

"Rehearsal finished early tonight," Verna began. "I had a hunch so, after everyone left, I stayed and hid behind the curtain. Sure enough, Bela Mezgar stayed too. I thought he was going to make another phone call. Instead, he walked backstage and opened the door to the basement. After he looked around to make certain no one was watching, he slipped through and shut the door behind him. So I waited awhile and then followed him."

"You didn't!" I gasped.

"How else was I going to find out what he was up to? Anyway, the light was on but he was nowhere in sight. I tiptoed down the stairs and into the front part of the basement where they store all the costumes, props, and scenery. I had plenty of hiding places."

"Where was Mezgar?" Huntley asked.

"There's a separate room in the back corner—the furnace room. I snuck up and peeked in the door. It was dark, but I could see Bela Mezgar looking at something hidden behind a huge old furnace. It was covered with sheets and he started pulling them off. It was a coffin!"

"Did he get in the coffin?" Huntley asked.

Verna shook her head.

"No, he just stood there running his hands over the wood and talking to himself in Romanian. Then he covered the coffin up again and left. I waited until I was sure he was gone and then I ran over here."

"Good work, Verna!" Huntley exclaimed.

While she told us her story, Verna had been busily eating the pieces of pepperoni off our pizza. I really hate it when people do that. They leave you with a bald pizza. But I was so proud of her right then that I even picked up the last piece and popped it into her mouth myself.

14

Sunday afternoon, the three of us were on our way to the BLT to check out Verna's coffin. The day was cold and we walked quickly against the wind. Huntley was wearing his autumn monster-hunting get-up again. With his trench-coat collar turned up and the wide-brimmed hat pulled down over his forehead, he looked grim.

"I asked my mom about Sonya Hanson," he said after awhile.

"And?"

"And Sonya's from Romania, just like Bela Mezgar. She came to this country as a young girl with her mother. They settled in Pittsburgh. Later she got married. She has a son who now lives in California. When her husband died last year, she moved here to Barkley."

"Just because she happens to come from Romania doesn't mean she's the mystery woman Bela Mezgar's been calling from the BLT," Verna protested.

"True," Huntley admitted. "But don't forget that she's a member of both the Chatham and the BLT boards. We know from Peggy Love that it was Mrs. Hanson who convinced the BLT to put on a play Bela Mezgar could star in. And I'll bet you all the hot fudge in Majersky's that she was the one who got Chatham to invite our vampire to the United States in the first place. The fact that she's also Romanian is just icing on the cake."

Huntley must have won the argument because Verna shut up, something she doesn't do very often. And then we were walking up the tree-lined drive to the Big Lake Theater. Usually it's such a pretty place but, on that gray and cloudy autumn afternoon, it looked lonely and spooky. I shuddered and wondered what terrible secret might be hidden there.

We tried several of the front doors before we found one that was unlocked. Inside it was deathly quiet. The theater even felt empty. Verna led us backstage to the basement door. We stepped through and quietly shut the door behind us. We didn't dare turn on the overhead light so we stood on the small wooden landing, staring and listening into the thick blackness of the basement below. Then Huntley switched on his flashlight and we crept down the stairs. At the bottom he shone the beam around. The storage part of the basement was just the way Verna had said. Props, pieces of scenery, and costumes were everywhere.

Staying close together, we made our way through the clutter to the door of the furnace room. Huntley led the way. I held my breath as the huge BLT furnace rose up out of the darkness like a monster. My heart told me to run, but my feet followed Huntley and Verna around it. I knew what was going to be back there, but I still gasped when I saw it. The coffin!

We stood staring at the plain wooden box in the thin beam from the flashlight. We had agreed that one of us would slowly lift the lid of that coffin. If Bela Mezgar was indeed lying inside, we would carefully lower the lid and go get Police Chief Murphy.

Verna stepped forward and reached for the lid. Suddenly I grabbed her arm. I hadn't planned on being a hero. It just came over me. Verna had already done something brave by finding the coffin. Now it was my turn.

I carefully placed my fingers under the lid and began to lift. I prayed it wouldn't squeak. Suddenly the lid jumped up all by itself! A hand shot out and closed over mine! So much for bravery. I shrieked and tried to jump back, but the powerful grip tightened and pulled me closer.

"Help! Help!" I screamed, as I realized with horror that I was going to be pulled into the coffin with the vampire.

15

Huntley grabbed me around the waist and began pulling me. Verna grabbed Huntley's waist and began pulling him. Back and forth, back and forth, we went. It was a deadly game of tug-of-war, and I was the prize.

Suddenly the hand let go of my wrist and the three of us went flying backward in a heap. We quickly untangled ourselves and ran for the furnace-room door. It was a miracle we didn't break our necks as we fought our way through all the junk that cluttered the storage room. Behind us we could hear the vampire coming on strong.

I reached the steps first and led the charge up. When I hit the landing, I lunged for the door and grabbed the knob. It wouldn't turn! Someone had locked us in!

"Help us!" I screamed, as I banged on the door. "Let us out!"

I turned and saw Huntley pulling the little cross out of his pocket.

"Stay behind me!" he yelled to Verna and me.

Holding the cross out in front of him, he stood at the top of the stairs. Verna jumped up beside him.

"Come and get us, you overgrown mosquito!" she hollered.

I stood with my back to the door and looked at Huntley, stoutly holding the little cross, and Verna, shaking her fist. I knew I was going to die, but I was going to die with two of the best friends a guy could have.

And then I was falling backward. Lights blinded me. Someone had opened the door! I found myself looking up into the surprised face of the BLT custodian.

"Mr. Quimbly!" I gasped, as Huntley and Verna, breathless, came running out into the light. They were followed in a few seconds by Mr. Pano. I remembered that Mr. Pano was in charge of building the props and sets for the play.

"Mr. Pano? Was that you in the coffin?" Verna asked in amazement.

"Of course," Mr. Pano said with a chuckle. "I was down there putting on the finishing touches when the lights suddenly went out. I thought one of the crew was playing a joke on me so I climbed in the coffin and waited. Sure enough, in a little while you kids came sneaking in. I thought *you* were trying to scare *me.*"

"But we didn't turn off the lights," I protested.

"I turned them off," Mr. Quimbly said, looking at Mr. Pano. "I didn't know you had gone down there so I thought *I'd* left them on."

"Did you also lock the door?" I asked.

Mr. Quimbly shook his head. "That door sometimes sticks if you turn the knob too hard."

"So that's the coffin for the *play?*" Verna asked.

Mr. Pano laughed. "What did you think it was? The real thing? The storage room is so crowded I have to work on it back behind the furnace. We'll be bringing it up to the stage soon."

For the first time, Mr. Pano seemed to notice the nervous looks on our faces.

"Say, I didn't really scare you kids, did I? You

knew who it was down there, didn't you?"

We assured him we had and made a quick exit before he could ask us any more questions.

"I should have known Bela Mezgar wouldn't try to hide his coffin in the BLT," Huntley groaned as we walked down to the edge of the lake. "It would be too risky."

"And I should have known that the coffin downstairs was for the play," Verna said, angrily throwing a stone into the water. "That's why Mezgar was down there checking it out."

"Look at it this way," I said, trying to cheer them up. "If the coffin in there had been the one we're looking for, we'd probably be trapped in that dark basement with the vampire."

That did the trick! Both Huntley and Verna sighed and then smiled.

16

Huntley said we needed time to relax and clear our minds. In a little while we were sitting in his office playing Monster Monopoly. It's a game Huntley invented himself. You play it just like regular Monopoly only with different names. You buy properties like Blobwalk and Psycho Place. Instead of going directly to jail, you go directly to the cemetery. Instead of a Community Chest, Huntley's game has a Community Crypt. I could think of better ways to relax from vampire hunting.

When it was time for the evening news, Huntley turned on his TV.

"Good," he said when the program ended. "Still no reports of anyone's having blood mysteriously drained from his body."

"Could we be wrong about all this?" Verna asked as she got up to leave.

"No." Huntley shook his head. "Vampires sometimes take only a little blood from a lot of people. They can go undetected a longer time that way. But, sooner or later . . . if they keep coming back for refills . . ." His voice trailed off spookily and I shuddered.

Before I left, I borrowed a vampire book. I figured if I learned as much as I could about vampires, it just might save my life one day.

That night I lay in bed reading until I knew more about vampires than I really wanted to know. I turned out the light and lay there listening to the wind moaning through the trees outside. Our house is a one-floor ranch style. My bedroom is at the corner of the house. My parents' and my little brother's bedrooms are at the other end of the hall. Usually I like being off by myself. Not that night.

A hard gust sent leaves swirling against the walls. The sound startled me. I sat up in bed and looked at the window. What I saw made me jump higher than the time Verna snuck up behind me in the school cafeteria and slid a square of orange jello down my back.

There was a face in my window. It was Bela Mezgar! His skin was that awful white color. His eyes were wide, dark, and crazy. He was smiling at me. It was a sickening smile. Slowly his mouth opened wide, and for the first time I saw the terrible fangs. His cape was swirling behind him like a black ghost and he was reaching for the window.

I let out a scream. If Peggy Love had heard that scream the night of the auditions, she would have given me the part on the spot. Suddenly my overhead light came on as Mom and Dad ran into the bedroom.

"I saw a face looking in," I said, pointing.

Dad ran to the window and peered out. Mom tried to calm me down.

"No one there now," Dad said.

"You just had a nightmare," Mom said, trying to reassure me.

Suddenly I wanted to tell them the whole awful story. After all, the vampire had actually been here at my house! My family was in danger. But I knew they wouldn't believe me. So I kept quiet and let them tuck me in again.

"It's that garlic powder he's been eating," I heard Mom tell Dad as they left the room. "Have you noticed how he's been sprinkling it on everything lately?"

17

"He's on to us!" Huntley exclaimed the next morning when I called him before school. "We have to move fast!"

"What's next?" I asked.

"Tonight we go out to Sonya Hanson's house. She's helping him carry out his evil plans. I'm sure of it. His new coffin must be out there!"

I shuddered. Bravery is not one of my strong points. Verna once told me that, on the Verna Wilkes' Courage Scale, I didn't even appear. But having the vampire come to my house had done something to me. We had to stop him before he could spread terror to our peaceful little town.

Huntley and I met at the public library that night and tried to concentrate on our homework. Then we headed out into the cold autumn evening. The opening night of the play was coming very soon. So was Halloween. Many of the houses had flickering jack-o'-lanterns on their porches. The round yellow faces seemed to be grinning evilly as if they knew what awaited us at the end of our hike.

Sonya Hanson had bought the old Brewster place out on Shady Lane. Huntley and I walked along the Washington Pike and turned left onto the old country road, where the houses were few and far between.

The Brewster place sits all alone in the middle of a field. It's a big red-brick farmhouse over one hundred years old. We stood behind the barbed-wire fence that ran along the road and looked at it. Although the yard around the house was tidy, the surrounding fields were overgrown. Behind the house, the southern edge of Lost Woods stretched into the distance on its way to the shores of Lost Swamp. The woods looked wild and spooky, as if waiting to swallow up the lonely farm.

After helping each other through the barbed wire, we kept low to the ground as we moved toward the house. We stopped and hid inside a small grove of trees and bushes at the outer edge of the yard. A car and a small truck were parked in the driveway. By the pale moonlight, we could see the truck had California license plates. A light was on in one of the front rooms of the house.

We waited and watched and watched and waited until my teeth were chattering from the cold. Nothing suspicious or sinister happened. In fact, nothing happened at all. I checked my watch. Rehearsal at the BLT was probably over by now, but there was no sign of Bela Mezgar. Maybe he wouldn't come here tonight. Maybe Huntley was wrong about Mrs. Hanson, and Bela Mezgar would never come.

Whoooooo! Whoooooo! Whoooooo!"

We heard what sounded like an owl with a beakful of M&M's.

"There's Verna," Huntley said. "*Whoooooo! Whoooooo! Whoooooo!*"

Huntley's owl was much better than Verna's. In a second, she was slipping into the bushes with us.

"Is Bela Mezgar coming?" I whispered.

Verna shrugged her shoulders.

"I'm not sure. Peggy Love wanted to talk to me about something after rehearsal so I lost track of him."

"He's here!" Huntley whispered excitedly.

Verna and I looked at the front door and the driveway. No one was in sight. Then we followed Huntley's gaze upward. I gasped. There, in the light of the moon, a bat was flying toward the house!

18

We watched in amazement as the bat swooped toward the roof and disappeared. A minute later, several more lights went on inside.

"What now?" Verna asked the question I would have asked if my tongue hadn't been stuck to the roof of my mouth.

"We have to see what's going on in there," Huntley answered. "Each of us will take a side and try to peek in. Raymond, you take this side. I'll take the far side. Verna, you try the front."

As Verna started to move out, Huntley grabbed her arm.

"Listen," he warned us. "Keep low and be careful. If one of us gets captured, the other two shouldn't try any daring rescues. Just run and get Police Chief Murphy."

I knew he was really warning Verna. He knows I'm not into daring rescues.

We fanned out to our posts. There was a light in one of the windows on the near side. I stood on tiptoe and peeked in. I saw a comfortable-looking dining room with antique furniture and a large stone fireplace. Much to my relief, the room was empty.

My relief didn't last. A light suddenly appeared at my feet. Startled, I jumped to one side.

There was a small narrow window at the base of the house I hadn't noticed before. I dropped to my stomach and peered down. The window was so streaked with dirt I could barely see through it. I knew I was looking into a corner of the basement. The foundation walls were made of ancient-looking stone. The floor was dirt. The tiny light was moving slowly across the dark basement all by itself!

I wanted to wipe the window so I could see better but I was afraid of giving myself away. Instead, I pressed my face as close to the pane as I dared. I squinted hard and, as the light got closer to the wall, I saw that it wasn't really floating. It was a candle, and it was being carried by a woman. The woman was Sonya Hanson.

And then another light floated up and joined the first. When I saw who was carrying the second candle, I had to clutch the grass to keep myself from getting up and running away. Bela Mezgar! Now he and Mrs. Hanson were standing there looking down at something. The coffin!

I watched in horror as Bela Mezgar lifted the lid and climbed in. As he lay inside, Mrs. Hanson slowly lowered the lid over him.

That was the straw that broke the Almond's back! I rolled away from the window, jumped to my feet, and ran as if the entire defensive line of the Pittsburgh Steelers were chasing me. I was back on the Washington Pike and halfway home before Verna and Huntley caught up with me.

19

"I was right about Mrs. Hanson!" Huntley exclaimed after I told them what I had seen in the basement. "She's helping our vampire. He has a coffin in Pittsburgh, and now he has one here in Barkley. He can be in either place and always be near one. And I'm afraid this may be only the beginning."

"What . . . what do you mean by that?" I asked fearfully.

Huntley looked thoughtful. "What if Bela Mezgar has no intention of returning to Romania? The United States is so much bigger. Here he can travel freely all around the country, acting in plays while searching endlessly for human—"

"Don't say it!" I stopped him before he could say the dreaded word.

"Before long," Huntley went on, "he'll have coffins hidden in cities and towns all through the States. If he keeps moving, no one will have time to suspect what he *really* is."

I snapped my fingers. "The truck in Mrs. Hanson's driveway! It had California license plates!"

"That's right!" Verna exclaimed. "When he's finished his dirty work here, he's probably going to Hollywood or someplace."

"And then who knows where he'll strike next?" Huntley wondered. "Miami? New York City? Dallas? The whole country is in danger."

"Well, *I* say he goes no farther than here!" Verna announced with determination. "Right?"

"Right!" Huntley exclaimed as he and Verna did a high five.

As we continued our walk back to town, we made plans for the next night. Huntley suggested that he and I meet Verna at the BLT after rehearsal. He wanted to see if Bela Mezgar returned to Pittsburgh or if he turned into a bat again and flew out to Shady Lane.

"If he goes to Mrs. Hanson's house and gets into his coffin, we have him," he explained. "We'll go to Police Chief Murphy and tell him what we know. Then we'll take the chief out there and show him the vampire in his coffin. That should be enough proof."

Tuesday evening after dinner, Huntley and I did our homework at the library and headed out to the BLT. As we walked among the parked cars toward the front doors, I saw something out of the corner of my eye that made me stop.

"What is it, Raymond?" Huntley asked.

"See that guy in that black car over there?" I whispered.

"You mean the man with the metal glasses?"

I nodded and told Huntley how I had run into that same man in the bushes down near the lake.

"It seemed he was hiding in there or something," I explained. "And look how he's hunched down behind the wheel. Like he doesn't want anyone to see him."

"Strange," Huntley agreed. "Let's wait for Verna out here so we can keep an eye on him."

We waited and so did the man. When rehearsal

ended, the cast and crew poured out the front doors. Verna came over to us.

"I thought you guys were going to wait inside so you could keep an eye on Bela Mezgar?"

"Something came up out here," Huntley answered. "Take a look at that man in the black sedan over there and tell me if you've seen him before. Don't stare, though."

Verna casually glanced over at the car and then nodded her head.

"Yeah, I've seen him around here. I figured he was just waiting to pick someone up. Come to think of it, I can't remember anyone's ever leaving with him."

Just then Bela Mezgar came out with Dr. Stevens. We watched the two men get into Dr. Stevens' car and drive away. Shortly afterward, the man with the silver metal glasses started his car and pulled out after them.

"I guess Bela Mezgar's going back to Pittsburgh tonight," I said. "Say! Do you think Dr. Stevens is one of his helpers?"

Huntley shook his head. "I don't think so. But I'll bet you all the slime in Lost Swamp that the guy in the car is mixed up in this somehow."

“Oh, no!” Verna groaned. “Don’t tell me we’re going to investigate him, too?”

“We don’t have time,” Huntley answered. “We’re just going to have to ask him.”

I looked at Huntley to see if he was kidding. He wasn’t!

20

"Are you sure this is a good idea?" I fretted the next night.

Huntley nodded his head. "That guy is following Bela Mezgar just as we are. We *have* to find out why."

"But what if he's one of Bela Mezgar's helpers? He could attack us or something."

"That's a chance we have to take, Raymond."

We were standing in the BLT parking lot. Bela Mezgar had just arrived with Dr. Stevens for rehearsal. Soon after, the man with the silver metal glasses pulled in and parked his car in a corner of the lot away from the lights of the building. After rehearsal started, he got out of his car and walked down the slope toward the lake. He was no lightweight but he moved as smoothly and silently as a cat on the prowl. We watched him slip into the bushes, where he would have a good view of the BLT's front doors.

"Come on!" Huntley hissed, as he pulled me down the slope.

We stepped into the bushes and looked around in astonishment. No one was there! Then, suddenly, two strong hands clamped down on the backs of our shoulders and spun us around. We found ourselves looking up into the face of our man. A cigarette dangled from his lips. The glow from the ash eerily lit up his face.

"Why are you following me?" he asked in a voice that was soft but menacing. I wasn't really surprised that he had the same accent as Bela Mezgar and Sonya Hanson.

I gulped when I realized that he was talking to me. This was the second time we had met in the bushes and he remembered me. Before I could faint, Huntley stepped between us.

"Good evening, sir," he said boldly. "My name is J. Huntley English, M. H., and this is my associate, Mr. Raymond Almond. May I present my card?"

With that Huntley handed the man his new business card. Using the glow of his cigarette, the man read it.

"What does this mean?" he asked.

"It means that I'm a monster hunter. You see, I know that Bela Mezgar is really a vampire. My friends and I are investigating him so we can expose him for what he is. It seems you also are following him. May I ask why?"

I held my breath, wondering if the man might envelop us in his powerful arms and crush us. I was relieved to see a faint smile flicker on his lips.

"My name is Stefan Goma. I guess you might say I am . . . uh . . . a monster hunter, too."

"I thought so!" Huntley exclaimed. "Please go on, Mr. Goma."

"You are right about Bela Mezgar. I have been trying to destroy him for years. When he left Romania for the United States, I followed him. I'll chase him to the ends of the earth if I have to!"

"And we'll go with you!" Huntley said excitedly. "We'll work together!"

"No!" Stefan Goma snapped. "This is not a children's game. Bela Mezgar is an evil creature of the night. You and your friends would not have a chance, pitted against him. You must promise me that you will leave this deadly business to me."

My hand shot up like a rocket on the Fourth of July. "I promise!"

"Good!" Stefan Goma smiled at us. "Now you must tell me everything you have found out about our vampire."

Suddenly we heard voices coming toward us. Huntley and I spun around and saw a group of actors walking down to the lake. There must have been a break in the rehearsal. When we turned back, Stefan Goma had vanished as silently as he had appeared.

As we walked home later, Huntley was very quiet. I knew he was mad that Stefan Goma had removed him from the case.

"A children's game!" I heard him mutter under his breath. "We are conducting a serious investigation!"

I didn't share Huntley's anger. In fact, I was relieved. With Stefan Goma on the scene, we could drop the case without worrying or feeling guilty. He certainly seemed like the kind of person who could handle a vicious vampire.

I was so relieved that I even tackled a little homework before bed. Until I remembered the conversation in the bushes.

I had promised Stefan Goma that I would butt out. Huntley hadn't promised anything!

21

The next day at school I told Verna what had happened while she'd been in rehearsal.

"I'm glad we're off the case," she said with a sigh. "It was getting boring."

I shook my head. Only Verna Wilkes could think a vampire hunt was boring!

After dinner that evening, I phoned Huntley. Mrs. English answered and told me he had gone out for some fresh air. I hung up and sighed. I knew Huntley had gone to Sonya Hanson's house for his fresh air. I wasn't surprised that he was carrying on the investigation alone. I knew he wouldn't sit back watching

Chiller Theater on TV and let Stefan Goma get all the glory.

I tried doing my homework but my mind kept going back to Huntley. My best buddy was out there somewhere in the dark. I imagined him fleeing from Mrs. Hanson's house with a huge bat right behind him. I saw myself running up and beating off the bat with a big stick. That did it! I may never win the Hero of the Year Award but I wasn't going to let Huntley face the unknown alone.

I told my mother I was going for a walk. Once outside, I ran all the way up the Washington Pike. I didn't slow down until I turned off onto Shady Lane.

That's when I began to think. What if Huntley really *had* only stepped out for a short walk? What if I was out here alone? I tried to take heart by reminding myself that Bela Mezgar would still be at rehearsal.

I walked around a bend in the lane and suddenly I wasn't alone. I stood frozen until I saw that the figure coming toward me was Huntley.

"Boy, am I glad it's you!" I said when I got my voice back.

Huntley seemed startled to see me. He just stood there looking as if he wanted to say something but couldn't think of anything.

"Well?" I finally said.

"Well, what?"

"What's going on at Sonya Hanson's house? I know that's where you were."

Huntley's voice sounded strangely distant. "Nothing. Nothing at all."

With that he continued on his way home. At first I was hurt. Then I was mad.

"All right!" I shouted after him. "*Don't* tell me. I thought we were in this together. I guess I was wrong."

Huntley didn't answer. He just kept on walking away. I was so mad I went home a different way.

Not until I was lying in bed that night did I *really* think about what had happened. I had known Huntley since our diaper days. He had never treated me like that before. I thought about how his voice had seemed faraway. And then I remembered his eyes. Even in the dark, they had seemed kind of glassy as if he were . . . hypnotized!

And then I knew something had happened to him out at Sonya Hanson's house. Something evil!

22

I caught up with Verna the next morning on our way to school and told her what had happened out on Shady Lane.

"Huntley was really acting weird," I said, finishing my story.

"That's because he *is* weird," Verna said with a snicker.

"This is serious, Verna! I think Bela Mezgar has him."

"Has him?"

"You know. Has him under his spell."

"There's nothing wrong with Huntley that a good dose of sanity wouldn't cure."

"Listen!" I persisted. "I'm going to follow Huntley tonight. Will you come with me?"

Verna shook her head. "No, I have the dress rehearsal tonight. The play opens tomorrow, you know."

With that she walked away. I had never felt so alone in my life. I wondered if I should tell Stefan Goma what had happened to Huntley. Then I realized I couldn't go looking for him and follow Huntley

at the same time. I decided to follow Huntley. I couldn't let anything more happen to him.

After dinner, I waited in the shadows across the street from Huntley's house. Sure enough, out he came and headed toward the Washington Pike. It was easy tailing him, since I knew right where he was going. He walked through the cold night as if he were a robot or something.

I followed him straight to Sonya Hanson's house. There were no lights on inside. There was no car or truck in the driveway. It looked as if no one was there. I wondered if maybe Huntley would turn around and go home. Instead, he stepped up on the porch and let himself into the house. Then a light came on.

Only one thing made me follow him. Friendship! I quietly shut the door behind me and found myself in a long hall. A lamp was lit on a table near the door. At the end of the hall, I caught a glimpse of Huntley disappearing through a door on the left. I tiptoed after him and found myself looking down a flight of steep narrow wooden steps. A faint light was glowing from somewhere below. I couldn't stand the cat-and-mouse game any more.

"Huntley," I called softly down the stairs. "Huntley. It's me, Raymond. Come up here."

The light below went out. He was trying to hide from me! I had come too far to turn back now. I decided I had to go down there and *drag* him home, if necessary.

Walking down those steps into the basement was like descending into a huge black mouth. "Huntley," I hissed into the darkness at the bottom.

By the light drifting down from the hall, I saw a flashlight and some candles and matches sitting on a table. I tried the flashlight. The batteries were dead so I lit a candle. The flame flickered eerily off the stone walls as I made my way across the dirt floor.

I knew right where to go. The corner I had looked at through the window. That's where I found the coffin. It was sitting in a pile of wood chips and tools.

I felt myself being drawn toward it as if I were under a spell. Slowly I lifted the lid. A scream tore itself from my throat!

How I got out of the house so fast I'll never know. One second I was staring into the coffin. The next I was running across the field. I was running so hard I almost knocked Verna Wilkes down.

"Raymond!" she said, shaking me. "What's the matter? I heard a scream."

"The coffin!" I shouted, pointing back at the house. "He was lying in the coffin!"

"Who was?"

"Huntley!" I gasped.

23

"Let's go get him out of there!" Verna said, starting toward the house.

"No." I grabbed her arm. "It's too late for that."

"What do we do then?"

"We go to the police. Now!"

We ran quickly back to town.

"Where did you come from?" I asked Verna. "And why are you dressed like that?"

"This is my peasant-girl costume. I told you tonight was a dress rehearsal. But, well, I . . . uh . . . was worried about you and Huntley. I told Dr.

Stevens I had to leave early. He wasn't very happy about it, but I said it was an emergency."

"How can I ever thank you, Verna?"

"By not thanking me!" she snapped.

We found Hank Murphy, the Barkley Chief of Police, sitting at his desk in the small police station downtown. Chief Murphy is a big man with short wavy hair and a bristly mustache.

"Verna? Raymond?" He looked at us in surprise. "I was just catching up on a little paperwork. What brings you here this time of night?"

Breathlessly we told him the whole terrible story from beginning to end. When we were done, the chief just sat there staring at us.

"Thank you for reporting this to me," he said after awhile. "I'll look into it."

We thanked him and stepped back outside.

"Do you think he believed us?" I asked Verna.

"Are you kidding?" she snorted. "We're lucky he didn't lock us up in a padded cell."

"Then *we* have to save Huntley!" I cried. "Let's go back out to Mrs. Hanson's!"

Verna grabbed my arm. "No, it really is too risky. We might end up like Huntley."

"Maybe Stefan Goma can help us?"

"Maybe, but we don't know where he is."

"But we have to do something!" I insisted.

"I have a plan," Verna said. "We're going to need help saving Huntley. But no one is going to help us unless we can convince them that Bela Mezgar is a vampire. So we're going to expose him in front of the whole town."

"How are we going to do that?"

"The play opens tomorrow night. Everyone will be there. At the end of the last act, Count Dracula crawls into his coffin and dies. That's when we'll strike!"

"Strike?"

"When Bela Mezgar climbs back out of the coffin to take his bows to the audience, you'll jump on stage and throw garlic powder on him. That should keep him busy while I tell the audience all about him. If they need more proof, I'll hold a mirror up to his face."

"A mirror?"

Verna nodded. "I've done some reading on vampires myself. They have no reflections in mirrors."

I had to admit that Verna made sense. Her plan sounded safer than rushing out to Sonya Hanson's house and maybe getting captured ourselves.

"So what do you say?" Verna asked. "Are you with me?"

"I'm in," I said doubtfully. "I just don't like waiting until tomorrow night to save Huntley."

Verna put her hand on my shoulder. "Huntley's going to be all right. Don't forget, you saw him going home last night. So they'll let him go tonight, too. They know if he doesn't come home his parents will call the police. Besides, he's under Bela Mezgar's spell. They know they can pull him back any time they want."

I nodded my head. As worried as I was about Huntley, I had to admit I liked the idea of confronting Bela Mezgar with lots of people around.

"Well, okay, then," I said. "That is, if Huntley really is home safe. Let's go call from the phone booth at Patsy's Pizza to make sure."

24

Verna was right. As I sat in the front row of the BLT the next night, it did seem that the whole town had turned out for the opening. I looked at the empty seat next to mine and felt bad. Huntley and I had planned to be there together. Now he was under the spell of a vampire. I felt a little better when I saw Chief Murphy and his wife take seats near me.

"*Psssssst!* Raymond!"

I looked up and saw Verna beckoning to me from behind the curtain onstage.

"What's up?" I asked as I joined her amidst the hustle and bustle backstage.

"Stefan Goma. I saw him in the parking lot earlier. I told him almost everything we know."

"Did you tell him what we're going to do at the end of the play?"

"No, that's going to be our show. Did you bring the garlic powder?"

I patted my jacket pocket. "I bought a brand new jar."

I returned to my seat. The audience grew quiet as the curtain opened and then applauded the set Mr. Pano and his crew had built. It looked just like the inside of a spooky castle. Dracula's wooden coffin sat on top of a long altar in the middle of the stage. Bela Mezgar swept into the lights and from that moment on he had the audience in the palm of his hand.

"Wait until they find out they've been watching the real thing," I thought.

Even though I was terrified about what Verna and I were going to do, I still found myself enjoying the production. Near the end of the final act, Dracula's evil helpers sneak into the nearby village and kidnap a peasant girl—played by Verna. They bring her to the castle, and that's when Verna gets her chance to scream. Even though I knew it was coming, I still jumped. She sounded like a cross between a police siren and a hundred fingernails scraping across a chalkboard.

Then there was a loud crash as a mob of villagers broke down the castle door. When the angry villagers came pouring into the room and came face to face with Dracula and his helpers, a big fight ensued. The fight ended when one of the villagers plunged a wooden stake into Dracula's heart. Everyone held their breaths as Dracula staggered around the stage and then crumpled into his coffin. When he was dead, Peggy Love, who played the peasant girl's mother, slowly shut the lid.

The lights dimmed and came back on. The audience applauded enthusiastically as the actors took turns bowing. Now it was time for the star to climb out of the coffin and take his bows. I jumped onstage. Verna edged closer.

Everyone was staring expectantly at the coffin. The lid remained closed. The applause died out, and the audience began to laugh. They thought it was a joke. The actors just stood around, looking confused. Gradually the house fell silent. No one seemed to know what to do.

"Something's wrong!" I heard Peggy Love say. "Let's get him out of there."

Those nearest the coffin tried lifting the lid. It

wouldn't budge. Now the audience was standing up to get a better view. More actors attacked the lid, but it still refused to open. Mr. Pano came running from the wings, carrying a crowbar. Police Chief Murphy jumped onstage to help.

"I built this thing," Mr. Pano grunted, as he strained to pry the top off. "There's no way it could get stuck like this."

Chief Murphy's added muscle did the trick and the lid flew open with a splintering crash. I leaned over the coffin, ready to start throwing garlic powder. What I saw made my mouth fall open.

The coffin was empty!

25

As we stared down into the vacant coffin, we saw that it wasn't *completely* empty. It contained a small tape recorder with a note attached to it.

Puzzled, Chief Murphy picked up the recorder and read the note aloud. It said: "Please push the play button and listen." Shrugging his shoulders, Chief Murphy did just that. Everyone gasped as the sound of Bela Mezgar's deep voice filled the theater.

"Ladies and gentlemen," we heard. "Please forgive my rude exit. I had no choice but to leave you this way, as I will explain. I was highly honored to lecture at Chatham College and also to perform here at the

lovely Big Lake Theater. I must confess, however, that it was my sister who arranged both invitations. You see, my real reason for coming to the United States of America was to seek political asylum and to become a citizen of your wonderful country. Unfortunately, from the moment I arrived, I have been kept under constant surveillance by agents of my country's secret police. I was told that if I made any move to defect, they would harm not only me but anyone who tried to help me. That is why my sister, my nephew, and myself had to use this charade to give myself time to work out a plan of escape. I hope when we meet again I can perform before you in complete freedom as an artist and a citizen of the United States of America."

As the tape ended, everyone began talking at once, except Mr. Pano, who was examining every detail of the coffin.

"Say!" Mr. Pano roared above the excitement. "This isn't the coffin *I* built! Look at this latch on the lid. That's how he locked himself in."

"And look here," Dr. Stevens pointed out. "There's another latch on the bottom."

He undid the second latch, and a section of the coffin floor gave way. We found ourselves looking down through the hollow altar to an open trapdoor. A spiral staircase led farther down to the basement. I knew enough about theater stages to know that many of them have trapdoors like this one.

"That's how he did it!" Dr. Stevens exclaimed.

Suddenly a lot of things began falling into place.

"So Sonya Hanson is really Bela Mezgar's sister," I said, looking at Verna in amazement. "And Stefan Goma isn't a monster hunter. He's a member of the Romanian secret police."

"Oh, my gosh!" she said, smacking her forehead. "And I told him everything! Even how to get to Mrs. Hanson's house!"

"What do you kids know about all this?" Chief Murphy asked us.

"We'll fill you in on our way out to Sonya Hanson's," I cried, grabbing his arm. "We have to hurry! We might already be too late!"

"All right," the chief said, as the three of us ran from the theater. "But just don't tell me any more about vampires!"

26

Verna sat in the front seat of the speeding squad car and told Chief Murphy what we knew about this strange case. I sat in back, my thoughts racing as fast as the car.

On the tape, Bela Mezgar had said that his nephew was helping him escape. I remembered that Sonya Hanson's son lived in California and that the truck in her driveway had California license plates. And then there were the coffins. Two of them! One, Mr. Pano had built in the BLT for the play. But a second look-alike coffin, with a trapdoor, had been built in Sonya Hanson's basement. They'd probably used the nephew's truck to switch the two. But the most important thing was that Bela Mezgar wasn't a vampire. He was an actor trying to escape from behind the Iron Curtain. As usual, Huntley had gotten himself mixed up in the thick of things. But what had *he* been doing in the coffin?

As we drove up to Sonya Hanson's farmhouse, I was relieved to see only two vehicles parked in front. One was Mrs. Hanson's car. The other was her son's truck. There was no sign of Stefan Goma's black sedan.

"We're in time!" I cried, as Verna and I led Chief Murphy into the house and through the front hall.

The cellar door was open and we could hear voices below. I led the way down the steps and back into the corner. By the light of a number of flickering candles, we saw Bela Mezgar, Mrs. Hanson, and a man who looked exactly like a younger version of Bela Mezgar standing together along the wall.

"We came to warn you!" I panted. "You're not safe here! Stefan Goma knows everything. We brought Chief Murphy . . ."

That's when I saw the fear in their eyes, and I knew we were too late. Stefan Goma was there. He must have parked his car in the woods. I hadn't noticed him standing in the shadows, pointing a pistol at his frightened captives. Just behind him on the floor sat the coffin Mr. Pano had made for the play. I wondered if we all would be in coffins soon.

"Please come in and join our little party," Stefan Goma said in a nasty voice. "Chief Murphy, put your gun on the floor—slowly."

We all did as we were told.

"Please," Bela Mezgar pleaded. "Do what you want with me, but let my family and friends go."

Stefan Goma laughed evilly. "You were warned not to do anything to embarrass your government. You failed to heed that warning. Now everyone will pay for your disloyalty."

And then I saw something strange going on behind Stefan Goma. The lid of the coffin was slowly rising. I had to fight to keep my mouth from falling open as I watched Huntley quietly crawling out.

I glanced over at Verna. Our eyes met. Again and then again, she moved her eyes from my face down to my jacket pocket and then over to Stefan Goma. I knew what she wanted me to do.

Slowly I reached into my pocket and unscrewed the lid of the garlic powder jar. Then I tipped the jar enough to let the powder spill out. While I was doing this, Huntley was inching on his hands and knees till he was right behind Stefan Goma. Luckily, the secret agent was too occupied with saying awful things to the grownups to pay any attention to us.

Suddenly Verna screamed. I mean, she *really* screamed! It made her scream at the BLT seem like a hiccup.

Startled, Stefan Goma spun toward us. That's when I pulled my hand out of my pocket and fired a handful of garlic powder right into his face.

Digging at his eyes, Goma dropped the pistol and staggered back. Verna helped him along by shoving him in the chest. With a cry, Stefan Goma fell over Huntley and landed right in the coffin.

Huntley jumped up, slammed the lid shut, and sat on it. Verna and I quickly joined him. Stefan Goma pounded and hollered but the three of us stayed put. Not until Chief Murphy recovered his pistol and took charge did we get up and do a high five.

27

Later, Huntley, Verna, Bela Mezgar, Mrs. Hanson, her son, and I sat in the dining room eating hot homemade apple strudel. Chief Murphy had taken Stefan Goma off to town but had promised to return later for answers and strudel.

"The story really begins back when the communist Iron Curtain fell around Romania," Bela Mezgar began. "Our mother wanted to flee to freedom. Our father couldn't bear to leave his beloved homeland. So Mother took Sonya and fled to the United States. I stayed behind with father."

"Mother and I ended up in Pittsburgh." Mrs. Hanson picked up the story. "Later, I married a wonderful man named Bill Hanson. Peter here is our only child. When Bill died last year, I felt I needed a change, so I moved to this farmhouse. I tried to keep busy. I was already a member of the Chatham College Board of Trustees, and when I came to Barkley I also became active on the Big Lake Theater Board. But I was still lonely. Peter was living in California, and I hadn't seen my brother in over thirty-five years. I knew Bela had become a famous actor, but I wanted our family together."

"I felt the same," Mr. Mezgar added. "Our father had died in the meantime. In Romania, artists do not have the freedom they have here. In the United States I could be a real actor. I wanted to live the rest of my life in freedom near Sonya."

"We communicated through the underground," Mrs. Hanson explained. "I told Bela I would use my influence on the Chatham College Board to get him invited to the United States. I hoped the Romanian government would not suspect an invitation from such a distinguished institution as Chatham. When it was agreed he could leave the country for a semester's time, I thought our plan had worked. I was wrong."

Bela Mezgar sighed. "It would have worked if I

had not been careless and stupid. When I arrived in New York City, I was met at the airport by a very personable young man. He told me that Chatham College had sent him to escort me around New York and later to get me on the right plane to Pittsburgh. He was—most convincing. Foolishly I told him I hoped to stay in America. He expressed delight and I asked him what I should do next. He told me to wait in my hotel room and he would send someone who would help me.

"When there was a knock at my door later, I expected a representative of your government. Instead, the man you call Stefan Goma walked into the room."

"You see," Mrs. Hanson pointed out, "that young man had not been sent by the college to escort Bela. He was working for the Romanian secret police. His job was to test Bela's loyalty to see if he could be trusted during his visit."

"And I failed the test." Bela Mezgar continued the story. "Stefan Goma said that I would be kept under constant surveillance until I returned to Romania. He made it very clear that, if I refused to leave the United States when my visit was over, I would suffer. That did not frighten me. But when he said that anyone who helped me would also suffer harm, *that* frightened me. I was glad no one knew I had family in the United States."

"Family who were not afraid to help!" Peter Hanson cried angrily.

"Yes, but we had to be so very careful," Mrs. Hanson said, patting her son's hand. "We even suspected that the telephone in Bela's Pittsburgh apartment was bugged."

"That's why they were using the BLT's pay phone to call back and forth," Huntley explained. "They were pretty sure that wasn't bugged."

Mrs. Hanson nodded. "After Bela had gotten word to me that he was under constant surveillance, I tried to think up a way we could give him a chance to slip away."

"And so you came up with the trick coffin escape plan?" I asked.

"Yes." Mrs. Hanson smiled. "You see, the Big Lake Theater had already selected *The Count of Castle Dracula* as the play for Bela to star in. I wondered if we could somehow use the play to buy him the time he needed to escape. I knew that the play ended with Bela closed in the coffin. I also knew that the BLT stage has a trapdoor."

"And we knew that the secret police agent following me would probably be in the audience," Bela Mezgar added. "We hoped he would never suspect that I would try to escape onstage in front of an audience. The plan appealed to the actor in me."

"Peter came from California to build the trick coffin," Mrs. Hanson explained. "It had to match exactly the one Mr. Pano was building for the play."

Verna snapped her fingers. "That's why Mr. Mezgar was checking out Mr. Pano's coffin in the BLT's basement the night I followed him."

And *I* realized it was Peter I had seen that night through the dirty basement window. He did look just like his uncle.

"We used my truck to switch coffins just before opening night," Peter explained. "And after Uncle slipped down through the trapdoor, I was waiting outside to drive him here. We were going to pick up Mother and head for California. Of course, when we arrived, we found Stefan Goma already here—with his gun."

I looked at Verna, who was trying hard not to look guilty.

"Goodness!" Mrs. Hanson exclaimed. "We need more strudel."

As I eagerly dug into my second slice, I felt such warmth and love in the room that it was hard to believe we ever had thought Bela Mezgar was a cold-blooded vampire.

28

Peter Hanson offered to drive us back to town.

"Now it's your turn to explain," I said to Huntley as we all stepped out onto the front porch.

"I wasn't about to let Stefan Goma scare me off," he answered. "I decided to continue my investigation. I snuck out here Thursday night and hid under the porch. Mrs. Hanson and Peter came out and talked about their final plans. I realized how wrong I had been about this case. Of course, I immediately stepped forward and offered my services."

Mrs. Hanson put her arm around Huntley. "We

told him absolutely not. We were afraid for his safety, but he wouldn't take no for an answer. He was a big help, especially when we switched the coffins."

"They swore me to secrecy," Huntley went on. "That's why I acted so strangely when you met me walking home from here. I'm sorry, Raymond, but I couldn't tell you anything."

"It's okay," I said, "but what were you doing in the coffin last night?"

Huntley shrugged his shoulders. "Trying to hide from you. I didn't know you had followed me until you called my name, down in the basement. I was afraid if you found me you'd ask me a lot of questions I'd promised not to answer. I hid in the coffin because I figured you'd be afraid to look inside. I was real proud of you when you did."

"But what were you doing in the coffin tonight?" Verna demanded. "Don't tell me you were in there all that time?"

"While Peter went to the BLT to pick up Mr. Mezgar, I thought I'd better stay here with Mrs. Hanson in case she needed me. When Stefan Goma suddenly showed up, I managed to hide in the coffin before he saw me. I stayed in there until the time was right to make my move. I don't want to see the inside of another coffin for as long as I live!"

"Mr. Mezgar?" Verna asked suddenly. "Why did

you get so upset when Huntley stuck that cross in your face at the BLT?"

Bela Mezgar shook his head. "What would you do if someone suddenly jumped out at you and thrust something metal in your face? I did not know it was a cross. For all I knew, it was a knife."

"I can't say I blame you," Verna admitted.

"And I felt so bad I could not accept your luncheon invitation or Raymond's invitation to eat spaghetti at his house," the actor continued. "I was afraid the secret police might begin to suspect you if I accepted. So many people tried to be friendly to me, but I felt I had to keep to myself for their safety."

"That will change now," Mrs. Hanson said to her brother. "And I'm going to put some color in your cheeks. Look how pale you are!"

Bela Mezgar laughed. "I guess I have always been what you would call a night person. We actors are like that. But there is going to be so much to learn and do that I can see I will have to change my habits."

"Say," I said to Huntley as a thought popped into my head. "What about the bat we saw out here that night?"

The monster hunter looked sheepish. "It must have been a real bat out looking for its dinner."

"And what about the night I saw Mr. Mezgar looking in my window at home?" I asked next.

Huntley smiled. "You must have fallen asleep and had a nightmare. Too much garlic, maybe."

"It certainly wasn't I," said Bela Mezgar, looking mystified.

"One last question, Mr. Mezgar." Verna sounded puzzled. "When I overheard you talking on the phone at the BLT, you asked if your coffin was ready. I understand about that now. But then you said, 'My one heart must die so the other may live.' What did you mean by that?"

Bela Mezgar's big eyes filled with tears.

"In a way, I do have two hearts, Verna. One heart loves Romania, my homeland. My other heart loves freedom. When I decided to leave my country, I felt as if my one heart was dying. But I knew it must, so my love of freedom could live."

That thought made us all quiet for a long while.

29

And so we wrapped up "The Case of the Visiting Vampire." It turned out that Stefan Goma, or whatever his real name was, had something called "diplomatic immunity." That meant that he could not be prosecuted for what he had done because he worked for the Romanian Embassy in New York City. He did get kicked out of the USA for good.

Bela Mezgar was given something called "political asylum." That meant he could stay in our country and be protected by our government. The *Observer-Reporter* newspaper did a big story on him, and Huntley, Verna, and I were mentioned for our part in helping him escape from a dangerous enemy agent. Lucky for us, the reporter who wrote the story didn't ask us how we got involved in the first place. It would have been embarrassing if people had found out that we thought poor Mr. Mezgar was a vampire.

Bela Mezgar did return to the Big Lake Theater to act in the play. Instead of running for only a week the way it was supposed to, *The Count of Castle Dracula* played to full houses for over a month. Every night the audiences gave Mr. Mezgar a standing ovation. When the play finally closed, he returned to Pittsburgh to finish his semester at Chatham College.

Mrs. Hanson then sold her house and she and her brother moved out to Los Angeles to be near Peter. Shortly afterward, Huntley got a letter from them. He and I were sitting in his office watching *The Muppet Movie* on TV. I had told Huntley that I wasn't into watching Chiller Theater for awhile.

"It says here that Mr. Mezgar is being offered all kinds of movie roles," Huntley said, reading the letter. "One studio even wants to do a movie version of his escape to freedom."

"Hey!" I exclaimed. "Maybe they'll want you, Verna, and me to play ourselves in it!"

Huntley looked thoughtful. "It's hard to imagine Verna Wilkes as a movie star."

"Yeah," I agreed. "I don't think Miss Piggy has anything to worry about."

We laughed long and hard.

About the Author

DREW STEVENSON was born on Christmas Day in Washington, Pennsylvania. He received a B.A. in English from Bethany College in West Virginia, and a Master's Degree in Library Science from the University of Pittsburgh. He works as an Adult Services Librarian in Ithaca, New York, where he is also the host of a local cable television show called "What's Happening?" Mr. Stevenson writes the mystery and suspense book review column for *School Library Journal* and is the author of *The Case of the Horrible Swamp Monster,* also published by Minstrel Books. He and his wife, Liz, share their home with Quincy, a very remarkable cat.

About the Illustrator

SUSAN SWAN was born in Coral Gables, Florida. She received a Master of Fine Arts degree from Florida State University. Ms. Swan has illustrated many trade and text books for children. She currently lives in Westport, Connecticut, and has a terrific collection of windup toys.